President Trump's Month
An Epistolary Novella

President Trump's Month

An Epistolary Novella

by Ron Leshnower

Hillocrian Creative

PRESIDENT TRUMP'S MONTH: AN EPISTOLARY NOVELLA
RON LESHNOWER

Hillocrian Creative LLC
P.O. Box 1248
Melville, NY 11747
www.hillocriancreative.com
info@hillocriancreative.com

ISBN-10: 0-9892911-3-8
ISBN-13: 978-0-9892911-3-2

Printed in the United States of America

Cover and book design by Ron Leshnower

First Edition: August 2016

10 9 8 7 6 5 4 3 2 1

Visit WWW.PRESIDENTTRUMPSMONTH.COM for more information.

This is a work of fiction. See the Preface and Disclaimer for more information.

For more information about Hillocrian Creative products, visit www.hillocriancreative.com and follow @hillocrian on Twitter.

For my patient family

Even if the world goes to hell in a handbasket, I won't lose a penny.

—Donald J. Trump
(as reported by the
Chicago Tribune,
March 12, 1989)

Table of Contents

Preface and Disclaimer   xv

Prologue   1
Background Casting Call Announcement
(PRIVATE CORRESPONDENCE, JANUARY 3, 2017)

Chapter 1   5
Inaugural Address
(OFFICIAL TRANSCRIPT, JANUARY 20, 2017)

Chapter 2   17
National Day of Toughness and Superiority
(PRESIDENTIAL PROCLAMATION, JANUARY 20, 2017)

Chapter 3   21
Statement from White House Counsel
(OFFICIAL RELEASE, JANUARY 21, 2017)

Chapter 4   23
Revocation of Certain Executive Orders
Concerning Furthering the Public Interest and
Keeping America Safe
(EXECUTIVE ORDER, JANUARY 21, 2017)

Chapter 5   25
Statement from the Press Secretary
on the President's Morning Activity
(OFFICIAL RELEASE, JANUARY 21, 2017)

Chapter 6   27
National Sanctity of Human Life Day
(PRESIDENTIAL PROCLAMATION, JANUARY 22, 2017)

Chapter 7   31
Press Gaggle by President Trump
Aboard Air Force One
(OFFICIAL TRANSCRIPT, JANUARY 22, 2017)

Chapter 8   37
President's Calls to Foreign Leaders
(OFFICIAL RELEASE, JANUARY 23, 2017)

Chapter 9   41
Establishment of the National
Made in America Advisory Committee
(EXECUTIVE ORDER, JANUARY 24, 2017)

Chapter 10   45
Statement by the President on
International Holocaust Remembrance Day
and the 72nd Anniversary of the
Liberation of Auschwitz-Birkenau
(OFFICIAL RELEASE, JANUARY 27, 2017)

Chapter 11   49
First Presidential Weekly Address
(OFFICIAL TRANSCRIPT, JANUARY 28, 2017)

Chapter 12   53
National Day of Excellence
(PRESIDENTIAL PROCLAMATION, JANUARY 28, 2017)

Chapter 13   57
President's Schedule
(OFFICIAL RELEASE, JANUARY 30, 2017)

Chapter 14   61
Statement on the Signing of the
Freedom to Display the American Flag
Amendment Act of 2017
(OFFICIAL RELEASE, JANUARY 31, 2017)

Chapter 15   65
Second Presidential Weekly Address
(OFFICIAL TRANSCRIPT, FEBRUARY 4, 2017)

Chapter 16   69
National Burn Awareness Week
(PRESIDENTIAL PROCLAMATION, FEBRUARY 5, 2017)

Chapter 17   73
President's Schedule
(OFFICIAL RELEASE, FEBRUARY 6, 2017)

Chapter 18   75
President Ronald Reagan Day
(PRESIDENTIAL PROCLAMATION, FEBRUARY 6, 2017)

Chapter 19   79
Readout of the President's Call with
Prime Minister Benjamin Netanyahu of Israel
(OFFICIAL RELEASE, FEBRUARY 10, 2017)

Chapter 20   83
National Inventors' Day
(PRESIDENTIAL PROCLAMATION, FEBRUARY 10, 2017)

Chapter 21   87
Third Presidential Weekly Address
(OFFICIAL TRANSCRIPT, FEBRUARY 11, 2017)

Chapter 22   91
Remarks by the President on
Antonin Scalia's Legacy at an RNC Event
(OFFICIAL TRANSCRIPT, FEBRUARY 13, 2017)

Chapter 23   95
President's Schedule
(OFFICIAL RELEASE, FEBRUARY 14, 2017)

Chapter 24   97
Victims of the Philadelphia
Courthouse Bombing and Market Shooting
(PRESIDENTIAL PROCLAMATION, FEBRUARY 16, 2017)

Chapter 25   99
Fourth Presidential Weekly Address
(OFFICIAL TRANSCRIPT, FEBRUARY 18, 2017)

Chapter 26   103
Letter to a Young Girl in
King County, Washington
(OFFICIAL CORRESPONDENCE, FEBRUARY 19, 2017)

Chapter 27   107
Amendment to Executive Order 13694
(EXECUTIVE ORDER, FEBRUARY 19, 2017)

Chapter 28   111
Declaration of National Emergency by
Reason of Certain Terrorist Attacks
(PRESIDENTIAL PROCLAMATION, FEBRUARY 20, 2017)

Chapter 29   115
Presidents' Day Press Conference
by President Trump
(OFFICIAL TRANSCRIPT, FEBRUARY 20, 2017)

Epilogue   121
Message of Unity, Hope and Determination
from the Acting Assistant
National Continuity Coordinator
(OFFICIAL TRANSCRIPT, FEBRUARY 23, 2017)

Appendix   125
Chronology of Events

Preface and Disclaimer

This book is a work of fiction, set in an imaginary future. It is an epistolary novella that tells a story with a sequence of documents rather than through a traditional narration.

Although the documents may appear realistic, they are not real. The use of real names, characters, organizations, governments, places, and incidents are for political satire and realism. Other names are fictional, and any resemblance to actual persons, living or dead, businesses, companies, events, or locales is entirely coincidental.

Whether you consider Donald Trump to be tremendous or a total and complete disaster, I hope this book entertains you.

—Ron Leshnower
AUGUST 2016

Prologue

Background Casting Call Announcement
(PRIVATE CORRESPONDENCE, JANUARY 3, 2017)

To: Casting List - MAIN
From: [redacted]
Date: Tuesday, 3 January 2017 8:14 AM
Subject: Exciting/Unusual Background Job Opportunity

Good morning!

We hope everyone had a happy and safe New Year! We are excited to inform you that we are helping out one of our associates with an awesome event happening on FRIDAY 1/20/17 in or around the Washington, D.C., area.

This is an event in support of patriotism and all that our country believes in, and it promises to be a very exciting and historic opportunity.

PLEASE NOTE! As a subscriber to this casting call email list, we remind you that the agreed-upon terms of service requires you to keep this email and its contents in the strictest of confidence, including from any and all media inquiries.

This event is code-named "Red Cap" and will be televised.

We are looking to cast people for the event to wear sweatshirts, carry placards and help cheer in support of a special announcement.

Please note that this is not a traditional "background job," but we strongly believe that acting comes in all forms and this latest opportunity is inclusive of that school of thought.

This event is happening LIVE and will require your presence and involvement from 7:45AM-1:30PM. LESS THAN 6 HOURS.

This will take place outside / exterior.

The rate for this is: $400 CASH at the end of the event.

We would love to book you if you are interested and available.

Please let us know and we will get back to you with confirmation.

Chapter 1

Inaugural Address
(OFFICIAL TRANSCRIPT, JANUARY 20, 2017)

Inaugural Address by President Donald John Trump

United States Capitol

11:56 A.M. EST

THE PRESIDENT: Thank you, everybody. Thank you. Thank you so much. Thank you. Folks, let me start with this…

First, I thank President Obama—No, no—I thank President Obama for his service to our nation. Thank you. I'm humbled. As I told Lesley Stahl in an interview on "60 Minutes," I'm a humble person—I'm much more humble than you would understand.

Okay, now that I've said that, let me say this, folks… My fellow Americans, our long national nightmare is over! You called for me, you wanted me, you fought for me, you nominated me, you elected me, and now here I am!

You know what we have now, folks? We have something in common. We love our country, we love our country, we just love our country. So we're gonna see some amazing things happen. Really beautiful things. Let me tell you, folks. We have a *real* rendezvous with destiny, and it's going to be tremendous, folks. Tremendous.

I didn't have to run. I mean, what did I need this for? Right? Why did I have to run? But I wanted to make America great. At the GOP Convention—remember the Convention?—we had four nights and four beautiful, strong themes. Make America Safe Again, Make America Work Again, Make America First Again, and Make America One Again. Beautiful themes. And they all add up to one thing—to Making America Great Again. I saw all the problems with this country, all the suffering, all the mismanagement, and I thought, somebody's gotta do something. So, here we are. We're here together. I am your voice! Let me tell you, it's a lovefest! Look at this crowd! It's beautiful!

One priority of my administration is to blot out terrorism all over the world. We have to defeat ISIS. And you know what, folks? We're gonna defeat ISIS. We're gonna do it. We're gonna stop the flow of terrorist immigrants into this country. We're gonna replace the "P.C. Police" with more of the real police. And we're gonna give the police all the respect they deserve, because —you know what?—all lives matter. They, frankly, do, folks. I was the law-and-order candidate, and I'm going to be the law-and-order president, folks. We're gonna share intelligence with the FBI, the CIA... And we're gonna make sure the Muslims speak up when they know there's a radical in their midst who's plotting an evil attack on innocents, on innocent civilians—including on Muslims, whom I love. I love everybody. I'm looking out for Muslims, too, folks. Nobody loves Muslims more than Trump!

And we have to very, very seriously talk about arming civilians— about arming them more. The whole Constitution is important. It's sacred. Whether we're talking about Article I, Article II, Article XII, or the 30th Amendment. But the Second Amendment to the Constitution is a fundamental right for all Americans. Crooked Hillary Clinton and her sidekick, Corrupt Kaine, wanted to repeal it and take away everyone's guns— everyone's guns except for the terrorists'. The terrorists could just come over here with their guns and start shooting. No more, folks! No more.

But we have to be armed, too. The good guys have to be armed, folks. Then these things wouldn't happen. You know, the movies... You shoot first, talk later. You talk about it later. Just make sure you shoot first. Why do we have to announce what we're doing? Why do you have to tell the enemy that we're sending people? America can't be so predictable. Predictability is vulnerability. It's no way to stay safe.

Get 'em out! Don't hurt the person… So disrespectful. So disrespectful. Treasonous. Just horrible. Get 'em out! Hey, your candidate lost! Who sent you? Crazy Bernie? Pocahontas? I always say, be nice to our protestor. Be gentle. Be very, very gentle. Don't hurt the person. Ah, he's got a friend over there… You know, your candidate lost! Go delete *your* account. Huh? Go delete your account, you (inaudible). Unbelievable. Unbelievable.

So, we also have to get tough with other countries. China, Japan, Mexico… Just about everybody is eating our lunch. When did we beat Japan at anything? They send over millions and millions of their cars. When was the last time you saw a Chevrolet in Tokyo? When did we beat China in a trade deal? But I beat China all the time. All the time.

We're gonna make great deals, folks. As sure as my fingers are long, we're gonna make great deals. I don't care if they're free, I don't care if they're fair, I don't care if they're good, I don't care if they're horrendous—I don't care what the heck they are, folks. I just want great deals. Great deals! I'll do it all different ways, folks.

And we're gonna be looking very carefully at that Iran deal, too. It's a total, total disaster, and we're gonna dismantle the disastrous Iran deal very soon. Iran is financing military forces throughout the Middle East, and it's absolutely, totally indefensible that we simply handed them over $150 billion to facilitate even more acts of terror. Recently, Iran has carried out terror attacks in 25 different countries on five continents. They've got terror cells everywhere and they're the biggest sponsor of terrorism around the world. We have to stop them and the evil that they spread and inspire. And we will stop them, folks.

Government can't allow this anymore. We finally have to do something. And we will. We will. Believe me.

It was 64 years ago today, I'm told… 64 years ago today when the great President Dwight Eisenhower delivered his inaugural address. And, by the way, on my eighth birthday—the day I turned eight—I remember this—President Eisenhower signed a law adding "under God" to our Pledge of Allegiance. This was 1954, folks. This was when America was truly great.

Anyway, in his inaugural, Eisenhower laid out nine principles for this great country. Principle 3 was this—let me read it to you: "Knowing that only a United States that is strong and immensely productive can help defend freedom in our world, we view our Nation's strength and security as a trust upon which rests the hope of free men everywhere. It is the firm duty of each of our free citizens and of every free citizen everywhere to place the cause of his country before the comfort, the convenience of himself."

You know, what's funny is I echoed this very thing in my book, *Crippled America*. I wrote, "Everything begins with a strong military. Everything." And I mean it, folks. We're fighting medieval barbarians—and we're in 2017! That's who we're fighting. And as the great, true American war general William Tecumseh Sherman said, "War is the remedy that our enemies have chosen, and I say let us give them all they want." Yes, let us give them all they want! Sure, diplomacy's great. But when it's time to stand up and fight, you've gotta fight. And you've gotta know when it's time to fight. And you can't be scared, folks. You can't let the terrorists win.

Clemenceau—that's an "E-A-U" at the end; I could never figure out French spelling!—said that war is too serious a matter to entrust to soldiers. Especially French soldiers, right? Ha, I'm kidding, I'm kidding! Yeah, pass the freedom fries. But we love the French. No one likes the French more than Trump. But, anyway, he's right. It starts at the top. With the decisions. And we're not just gonna shoot and bomb all over the place. I mean, I want to bomb the hell out of ISIS, but we're gonna be fair, we're gonna be reasonable. We're gonna always pursue peace and peaceful options. I love peace. No one loves peace like Donald Trump. We're gonna try peace, and we're gonna try diplomacy. But the truth is, folks… When these things don't work, that's when we bomb. That's when we bomb. And maybe I'll get my second Purple Heart. You never know.

What's this? Who's that? Excuse me, sir. Are you friend or foe? Friend or foe? Okay, he's a friend. He's good. Glad to have you. Glad to have everybody here. He's another one of my African-Americans. Hey! Are you the greatest? You know what I'm talking about! We have tremendous African-American support. Tremendous. And the reason is I'm gonna bring jobs back to this country! I love everybody, folks. Everybody.

Anyway, speaking of France, you know Paris has, they say, the toughest gun laws in the world. But that didn't stop the horrible attacks last year. Actually, it helped enable them, folks. Because no one was armed—no one except for the terrorists. And, you know, the press—the press calls the Paris terrorists "masterminds." I call them thugs. You can't call them masterminds. That's why every kid around the world wants to join ISIS now. They want to be a mastermind. Because it's great to be a mastermind. It's amazing, folks. Amazing. Kids used to grow up wanting to be an American astronaut, a firefighter, policeman, maybe a teacher… but now the kids want to run away and join ISIS. It's disgusting. Or they want to be a lone wolf like that Tunisian guy in Nice. It's disgusting. It's truly disgusting. And it's gonna change, folks. It's gonna change.

Let me tell you, it's going to continue to get worse until they respect us, folks. They have no respect for us whatsoever. We're trying to be nice. Saddam Hussein was a bad man—I've said this all along but the media ignores me—he was a bad man. But he knew how to get the terrorists. You know why? Because he wasn't nice. He was a bad man! So we have to identify the problem. We have to identify the problem and use the term "radical Islamic terrorism." We can't be politically correct. We can't afford to be politically correct anymore. It's either be polite to the bad guys or lose American lives. It's that simple. It's that simple, folks.

So, anyway, you know, it was a tough road here. Starting with that slow escalator ride at Trump Tower. It was like a slow-motion ride—wasn't it the greatest? It was a really tough road, though. Really tough. No one predicted I would make it this far. Absolutely no one. I had to beat 16 professional establishment politicians in the primaries. Lyin' Ted, Little Marco—you know, the guy who kept saying he won after finishing third? Unbelievable!—you know them all… But, you know what? Not only did I win, but I got more votes—almost 14 million votes, can you believe it?—than any other candidate in the history of the Republican Party! More than Reagan, more than Nixon, more than the Bushes. My supporters—my fans—are so loyal. Even David Duke, who I totally and completely disavow, by the way. As I said a year ago at a South Dakota rally, I could stand in the middle of Fifth Avenue and shoot people and I wouldn't lose voters. I didn't test it out, but I was right. Then I had to beat Crooked Hillary—certified "crooked" by FBI Director James Comey—Crooked Hillary, who—true to her name—stole the nomination away from Crazy Bernie. She totally stole it, folks, with the superdelegates and the rigged system run by Debbie Wasserman Schultz. I was the first to call it the rigged system. Rigged! That's what it is. The cards were stacked in her favor before the primaries even began. If I were a Bernie supporter, I'd feel absolutely disgusted. Totally disgusted. It's a rigged system. A rigged system.

But then, Crooked Hillary short-circuited. She said it herself. She short-circuited—I can't even say it, it's like a tongue-twister! So, I made it here, folks, despite the horrible media, despite the brilliant pundits and the know-it-alls who know everything (except, to be honest, for the fact they know nothing), and despite the naysayers. To paraphrase One Corinthians 9:24, you know, every runner in a race runs—every runner runs—but only one gets the prize. Only one.

Speaking of brilliant people, these self-proclaimed brilliant people have criticized Donald Trump for how he speaks, saying he talks about himself in the third person.

People have criticized Donald Trump for doubling down. Well, not only don't I double down, but I've never doubled downed. And if someone challenges me on this, I'll say it even stronger next time. Believe me.

People—these even more brilliant language eggheads—have criticized Donald Trump for winning the election by using certain specific "rhetorical devices," as they call it. And they've got all these fancy names. Like apophasis. Apophasis? You know what? I'm not even going to go there. Won't even talk about that, folks. Or anacoluthon, which means—you know, it's horrible. Or hyperbole—and this is a huge one, folks—which they accuse me of doing millions and millions and millions of times. Or epizeuxis, which I think sounds like "loser" but the truth is we're gonna win, win, win!

Have I lost you? You know what, who the heck wrote this stuff? This is what happens when you rely on a teleprompter. And when you rely on these nerds, these speechwriters who think they're funny, just trying to help you out. I feel kind of like I'm in a book about Trump. I'll be in many books, folks. Let me tell you. The best books. You know, I hate using a teleprompter. I like using my own words. But now I'm a politician. So I gotta use them—I've gotta use them, folks—but only sometimes. I promise you, I'll still be Trump. No matter what, I'll still be Trump.

But you know what, folks—this all just proves that you can win —even the presidential election—but you just can't win over everybody. And that's okay! I don't need everyone's support or endorsement. I didn't change when I became the Republican nominee and I'm not going to change as president. Why should I? This is who you elected. Right? And, don't worry, the stock market is going to totally rebound. The Dow Jones is going to go through the roof once I get to work and change this country.

I'm gonna be a different kind of president. A great one, folks. I've been elected to break up the establishment and change the status quo. As Thomas Jefferson wrote to James Madison: "I hold it that a little rebellion now and then is a good thing, and as necessary in the political world as storms in the physical." So, that's a good thing, folks.

And, let me just say, don't worry, progressives—there's something here for you. We're gonna fix the environment, folks. We don't need more regulations… we need less. Fewer! I'm very well educated, folks. I went to an Ivy League school. There's no one as good at grammar as me, folks. Believe me. Take California. There's no doubt that there's no drought, folks. It may rhyme, but it's true. The incompetent government's not looking out for the people. They're taking the water and shoving it back out to sea. They're trying to save a certain kind of three-inch fish. In the meantime, the farmers are hurting—thanks to the corrupt, incompetent career politicians.

Speaking of making history, I'm gonna make history right now. I'm gonna be the first president to personally live-tweet his inauguration speech. Watch this! Take out your phones. Maybe in four years, at my next inauguration, they'll all be made in America, not China. There! I'm gonna read you this tweet for the record here: "Looking forward to being POTUS. Will make America great again and build a beautiful wall. Exciting! #trump2016 #trump2020"

And I'm also gonna make presidential history again by taking a selfie during my inauguration speech. Here we go… There! Great. And I'm gonna tweet that selfie in a minute…

So, I don't know if you've heard me mention it, but we're gonna build a wall. Have you heard me mention that? We're gonna totally build a wall, folks. Of course, you've heard me say that so many times and now we're really gonna do it. The "Great Wall of Mexico!" Mexico's gonna pay for it, you know. Mexico's gonna pay for it, so they can have naming rights. If they want. I don't know. Or we can put a big "Trump" on it. What do you think? Huh? Everything's negotiable. Everything's negotiable, let me tell you. No matter what, I can tell you this, folks: it's going to be tremendous. Tremendous. Mexico is laughing at us, at our stupidity, and they're beating us economically. They're killing us economically. They're not our friend, folks. But, believe me, things are going to change. Believe me. We have no protection at our borders and we have no competence. We don't know what the hell is happening. It's got to stop and it's got to stop fast. And it will stop, believe me.

And we're gonna seriously look into implementing bans on Muslims or—or—people from certain countries that are horrible places. Really horrible places. We have to put a stop to it until such time as we can figure out what's going on. Now that I'm president, let me tell you… we will figure out what's going on.

We will figure out what the hell is going on. We have to help and take care of people, but we have to be smart. We're gonna destroy ISIS. ISIS has the oil, and what they don't have, Iran has. I warned, I said, "Don't hit Iraq" because we would totally destabilize the whole Middle East. But we did and now the oil is gone and the place is a mess. It's a huge breeding ground for ISIS. We can't even go to Iraq. Every time we give them equipment, the first time a bullet goes off, they run. They leave the equipment. Humvees, big vehicles. All for the enemy. We can't keep doing this, folks.

And we're being totally eaten alive with jobs. Our jobs are being taken out of the country. Our real unemployment is around 20 percent, folks. Maybe higher. And nobody talks about it. People —people just want their jobs back. They want their wages to go up. They want to manufacture things again. They want our country to do great things. Is there anything wrong with that, folks?

You're going to see, I will be the greatest jobs president that God has ever created. The greatest jobs president! I'll bring back our jobs from China, from Mexico, from Japan, from so many places, folks. China is devaluing their currency to a level that you wouldn't believe. It's been totally impossible for our companies to compete. Impossible, folks. But I'll bring back our money. We owe China over a trillion dollars. We owe Japan even more than that. So, you know what? Japan comes in, they take our jobs, they take our money, and then they loan us back the money, and we pay them in interest! And the dollar goes up so their deal's even better. How stupid! How stupid are our leaders for letting this happen? They don't listen to the American people. The people are saying, "I just want a job. I don't want talk. I want a job. I just want a job." Well, I'm going to be the greatest jobs president that God has ever created. You're gonna get your jobs. We're gonna open the floodgates, folks. Jobs are going to start flowing back inside our borders, believe me.

I hope you're ready, America. I hope you're ready to win, win, win! We used to do a lot of winning. But, for some reason, that stopped a long while ago. We've been low-energy. We've been like Jeb—remember him? That exclamation point at the end of his name didn't give him energy. But now that Trump is president, I'm telling you—I'm warning you—we're gonna win again, folks. Soon, you'll say, "Please, please, it's too much winning. We can't take it anymore! Mr. President, it's too much." And I'll say, "No, it isn't!" And you'll say, "We've won so much! How can we win more? It's too much winning. We just can't take it!" And I'll still say, "No, it isn't!" Because if America is going to be great again, we've gotta win, and we've gotta keep on winning. We can't stop winning, we just can't stop winning, and as long as I'm seated in the Oval Office, we won't stop winning! Because winning is all that we deserve and winning is all that we're gonna do, folks! (Applause.)

And just to make sure there's no misunderstanding here, let me say it again! We're gonna win, win, win, win, win!

Thank you! God bless you. And God bless the United States of America. America First! America First! (Applause.)

END
12:18 P.M. EST

Chapter 2

National Day of Toughness and Superiority
(PRESIDENTIAL PROCLAMATION, JANUARY 20, 2017)

Proclamation 9557 of January 20, 2017

National Day of Toughness and Superiority

By the President of the United States of America

A Proclamation

As I take the sacred oath of the highest office in the land, I am humbled by the responsibility placed upon my shoulders, renewed by the courage and decency of the American people, and fortified by my faith in a tremendous God.

America is at a crossroads. FDR said that "there are many ways of going forward, but only one way of standing still." I say, do we continue to stumble along in apologetic mediocrity, do we have our president run around the world on an apology tour while his country is floundering, or do we find the way back to renewed greatness and superiority?

Today, I took the presidential oath, a totally sacred oath, because you, the people, chose me to be your leader. And, in so doing, you made your decision loud and clear. You chose greatness and superiority for America. America first. Under my leadership, America will be great once again. And America will be the leader in all ways and in all times.

On this Inauguration Day, I ask that every American gather together in solidarity and greatness as we attempt, in the words of President John F. Kennedy, to "[l]et every nation know, whether it wishes us well or ill, that we shall pay any price, bear any burden, meet any hardship, support any friend, oppose any foe to assure the survival and the success of liberty."

NOW, THEREFORE, I, DONALD J. TRUMP, President of the United States of America, by the authority vested in me by the Constitution and laws of the United States, do hereby proclaim January 20, 2017, a National Day of Toughness and Superiority and call upon the citizens of our Nation to gather together in homes and places of worship to pray alone and together and offer thanksgiving to God for all the blessings of this great and good land. On this day, I call upon Americans to recall all that once made America great. Let us become not a nation that constantly engages in apology tours and displays of weakness, but a nation known for its toughness, a nation that is truly second to none in all respects. Let us ask our Heavenly Father for His guidance upon our Nation and its leaders in every level of government. With God's help, we will indeed make America great again.

IN WITNESS WHEREOF, I have hereunto set my hand this twentieth day of January, in the year of our Lord two thousand seventeen, and of the Independence of the United States of America the two hundred and forty-first.

ᗺᗺᗺᗺᗺᗺ

DONALD J. TRUMP

Chapter 3

Statement from White House Counsel
(OFFICIAL RELEASE, JANUARY 21, 2017)

Statement from White House Counsel

THE WHITE HOUSE

Office of the Press Secretary

For Immediate Release
January 21, 2017

The following is a statement from White House Counsel.

"We believe that the oath of office was administered effectively and that the President was sworn in appropriately yesterday. But the oath appears in the Constitution itself. And out of an abundance of caution, because there was a series of disruptions by unpatriotic and disgusting protesters during the first, second, and third iterations, Chief Justice Roberts administered the oath a fourth time this afternoon in a closed ceremony in the White House's Blue Room."

THE WHITE HOUSE, January 21, 2017.

Chapter 4

Revocation of Certain Executive Orders
Concerning Furthering the Public Interest and
Keeping America Safe
(EXECUTIVE ORDER, JANUARY 21, 2017)

Executive Order 13751 of January 21, 2017

Revocation of Certain Executive Orders Concerning Furthering the Public Interest and Keeping America Safe

By the authority vested in me as President by the Constitution and the laws of the United States of America, and in order to eliminate actions that do not serve the public interest or further our national security, it is hereby ordered as follows:

Section 1. Executive Order No. 13491 of January 22, 2009 (prohibiting enhanced interrogation techniques), Executive Order No. 13492 of January 22, 2009 (requiring the closure of the detention facility at Guantanamo Bay), and Executive Order No. 13493 of January 22, 2009 (establishing a special interagency task force on detainee disposition with armed conflicts and counterterrorism operations), are revoked.

Sec. 2. The heads of executive agencies shall promptly revoke any orders, rules, or regulations implementing Executive Order No. 13491 of January 22, 2009, Executive Order No. 13492 of January 22, 2009, or Executive Order No. 13493 of January 22, 2009, to the extent consistent with law.

Donald J. Trump

The White House,
January 21, 2017.

Chapter 5

Statement from the Press Secretary
on the President's Morning Activity

(OFFICIAL RELEASE, JANUARY 21, 2017)

Statement from the Press Secretary on the President's Morning Activity

THE WHITE HOUSE

Office of the Press Secretary

For Immediate Release
January 21, 2017

Below is a statement from the White House Press Secretary.

At 8:15 AM, the President arrived in the Oval Office and spent 10 minutes alone in the office. He inspected the room's decor, jotting down notes for its "total and complete" overhaul. While pausing in front of Childe Hassam's *Avenue in the Rain*, he wrote, "Beautiful. Absolutely beautiful. Amazing patriotism. This is what a great America looks like. Truly beautiful." Upon viewing *Cobb's Barns, South Truro* and *Burly Cobb's House, South Truro*, two Edward Hopper paintings on loan from the Whitney Museum of American Art, he wrote, "Boring, depressing, sad. Must go!"

The President then read the note left to him by President Obama that was in an envelope marked "To: #45, From: #44. Subject: Let's Keep America Great." At 8:25 AM, the White House Chief of Staff came in to discuss the schedule of today's events. The First Lady came into the Oval Office at 9:25 AM. We will tweet pictures and more shortly.

Chapter 6

National Sanctity of Human Life Day

(PRESIDENTIAL PROCLAMATION, JANUARY 22, 2017)

Proclamation 9558 of January 22, 2017

National Sanctity of Human Life Day

By the President of the United States of America

A Proclamation

This Nation was founded upon the belief that every human being is owed a promise of life and liberty. The visionary signers of the Declaration of Independence recognized an essential human dignity attached to all persons, no matter how frail or powerless, by virtue of their very existence. Every single person, including every child, whether healthy, wanted, or convenient, is a gift from our Creator and must be totally protected under the law.

Yet 44 years ago today, on January 22, 1973, the Supreme Court of the United States struck down our laws protecting unborn children. Since that time, the terrible toll of millions of innocent human lives has weighed heavily on the conscience of America.

So, we must commit to the pursuit of a more welcoming and compassionate society. We must forever reject the notion that certain lives are less worthy of protection than others. If lawmakers in California can create a drought by diverting millions of gallons of water to save a certain kind of three-inch fish, then surely we can commit to ensuring the viability of all human life.

Also, if Congress were to pass legislation making abortion illegal and the federal courts upheld this legislation, or any state were permitted to ban abortion under law, then only the abortion provider who performs this illegal, horrible act upon a woman would be legally responsible. The woman—and we cherish women—is a victim, along with the life that was in her womb. Academically, the woman would also be punished. But realistically, she should not be. We cherish women, folks. My position—pro-life with exceptions—has never changed and reflects the values and compassion of our late great president Ronald Reagan.

Finally, time and again, we have seen radical Islamics displaying their total lack of regard for the value of life. We are engaged in a fight against evil and tyranny to preserve and protect life. In so doing, we are standing again for those core principles upon which our great Nation was founded.

NOW, THEREFORE, I, DONALD J. TRUMP, President of the United States of America, by virtue of the authority vested in me by the Constitution and the laws of the United States, do hereby proclaim Sunday, January 22, 2017, as National Sanctity of Human Life Day. While the third Sunday of January has been traditionally selected, I find that this year, it is appropriate to mark the actual anniversary of the Supreme Court decision. I call upon Americans of all faiths and political affiliations to reflect upon the sanctity of human life. Let us all recognize the day with appropriate ceremonies in our homes and places of worship, rededicate ourselves to compassionate service on behalf of the weak and defenseless, and reaffirm our commitment to respect the life and dignity of every human being.

IN WITNESS WHEREOF, I have hereunto set my hand this twenty-second day of January, in the year of our Lord two thousand seventeen, and of the Independence of the United States of America the two hundred and forty-first.

DONALD J. TRUMP

Chapter 7

Press Gaggle by President Trump
Aboard Air Force One
(OFFICIAL TRANSCRIPT, JANUARY 22, 2017)

Official Transcript

Aboard Air Force One
En Route Joint Base Andrews

January 22, 2017

8:45 A.M. (local)

THE PRESIDENT: I want to make sure Americans know where I stand on certain things. Today is the anniversary of Woodrow Wilson's "Peace Without Victory" speech. He was basically trying to get everybody—all the European countries—to settle, folks. But it didn't work. You know what happened? A couple of months later, we declare war on Germany. It reminds me a bit of Brexit—which I totally called, by the way.

Q   So, what's the moral of this story?

THE PRESIDENT: You can't be nice, folks. You can't be soft. Not to terrorists, not to Nazis, not to Rosie, not to Megyn Kelly, not to the Zika mosquitoes, not to anybody. You just can't be a nice guy. You remember that song, that poem I recited all the time during the campaign? Let me tell you, I can't recite it enough. The one about the snake and the woman?

Q   How can we forget?

THE PRESIDENT: Well, it's all about "I told you so." The woman was nice, she let the snake in, and what happened? The snake bit her. But she knew the whole time he was a snake. So what does she expect? She was nice, but probably a nasty woman. A very nasty woman. That's just what I think. And she let the snake in, and she got what was coming. She got what was coming to her. America can't be nice and then have another

World Trade Center happen. We'll have more and more World Trade Centers, folks. There's no "I told you so." There'll be no one around to hear it. We can't have it. Remember the Orlando shooting last year with the gays? The LTG—LBGT—whatever it is—I immediately tweeted an "I told you so" not because I wanted praise—in fact, I specifically said I didn't want any congratulations. That's not the time to pat yourself on the back. But I wasn't President then. I couldn't do anything. Now that I'm President, I'm in a place, in a position, to stop these horrible acts —whether they're acts of terrorism, hate crimes against the gays, the Jews, the blacks, the Mexicans, whatever they are. There's no one more against discrimination than Trump.

Q   How will you stop horrible things from happening?

THE PRESIDENT: Through policies. And through being tough. Tough talk, tough action. And we've got to strengthen the Second Amendment. Not repeal it. Not limit it. Strengthen it. Good guys with guns means bad guys with guns die. It's that simple. And the other thing I wanted to say—you know, President Woodrow Wilson, he was a horrible president. He started the income tax, folks! And Barry Goldwater—remember him?—Barry Goldwater said, "The income tax created more criminals than any other single act of government." He was right.

Q   [LAUGHTER] Are you saying you're going to do away with income tax?

THE PRESIDENT: And put all the accountants and everybody out of work? No way. I'm a jobs president! I'm the greatest jobs president God has created. And taxes aren't bad. Not all bad. But it's not about good or bad. When it comes to taxes, it's not about good or bad. You know what it's about? It's about fair. Are you paying too much? Or are you paying too little? I'm going to meet with Senate leaders in the next week and talk about putting together a new comprehensive income tax reform so we can figure out what the hell is going on with taxes in this country and make sure everyone pays what's fair. Not just people, but the corporations. And also that they do pay. You know what? The audits aren't working, folks. They're scaring people. Good people. Small business people who are just trying to earn an honest dollar. And it's costing millions of dollars of wasted revenue. Millions, folks. And we're gonna fix that, too.

Q   Speaking of anniversaries, today's your 12th anniversary. Congratulations to you and the First Lady!

THE PRESIDENT: Thank you. Thank you very much. You're very kind. Sometimes a sleaze, but today you're very kind. And I would never make fun of disabled reporters, by the way. For the record, I never have.

Q   What are you getting the First Lady?

THE PRESIDENT: Well, you know what the 12th anniversary gift is, traditionally? It's silk. Beautiful silk. Soft silk. The greatest. So, I'll leave that to your imagination.

Q   [LAUGHTER] What are your anniversary plans?

THE PRESIDENT: Well, the moment we land I'm going straight to the Residence and telling them to hold all calls. I'll entrust the nuclear football to the Vice President for a little bit. The world can operate without me for just a little bit, I think. Pence is a competent guy.

Q   And the rest of the day?

THE PRESIDENT: It's all a surprise. But maybe we'll watch *Citizen Kane* in the Family Theater. Great picture. As I said

34

during my campaign, as President, you can't be predictable. And that's true as a husband. And in business. All my wives loved me —we had a great relationship. Every single one of them. Even if they didn't love me, they couldn't—not a single one of them— they couldn't say Trump was predictable. Trump's gonna do this, Trump's gonna do that. No one knew what the hell I was going to do next. Sometimes, even Trump didn't know what Trump was going to do next. You think I planned to give out Lindsey Graham's cell number on live TV? I just happened to have the card with me. In power and in love, you've got to be spontaneous, folks. You've got to keep the countries and the women guessing. I doubt Lyin' Ted keeps Heidi guessing. It's probably the same boring stuff every day. Or he promises her something but then he lies! He lies! I told Bill O'Reilly a while ago, I told him, "Bill, I'm gonna do what's right. I want to be unpredictable." And I told him voters don't want to know what I'm up to. They want unpredictable. And also I treat women—all women—with the greatest respect. My mother was a woman. I have daughters and they're women. Without women, nobody would be here—men or women. So, we've got to cherish them. We cherish women. Nobody loves women like Trump. And let me say this: at my wedding—and it was a beautiful wedding, by the way. Billy Joel was there and made up words about Trump. All the celebrities came. Even Crooked Hillary and Bill came. And back then, I said that I think it will be very successful, our marriage. And you know what? It was and it is and it will be. And I'm going to treat America like one of my precious wives. We're gonna be very successful, folks. It's gonna be beautiful. Trump and America, it's gonna be a beautiful marriage.

END
8:51 A.M. (local)

Chapter 8

President's Calls to Foreign Leaders
(OFFICIAL RELEASE, JANUARY 23, 2017)

President's Calls to Foreign Leaders

THE WHITE HOUSE

Office of the Press Secretary

For Immediate Release
January 23, 2017

This afternoon, President Trump had friendly, productive calls with one former and four current foreign leaders.

Former Prime Minister David Cameron, United Kingdom. President Trump said he regrets not being able to work with the former Prime Minister. He offered President Trump advice on growing the special relationship between our two countries in a post-Brexit world. He told the former Prime Minister that he loves England even though "America won that war" and that he still has tremendous respect for King George III for once saying, "I wish nothing but good; therefore, everyone who does not agree with me is a traitor and a scoundrel." After insisting that he wanted no credit for being right for predicting Brexit, the President also admitted that the EU referendum was not something he followed very much and suggested that his coincidental arrival in Scotland for the grand reopening of his Turnberry golf resort may have jinxed the vote.

Prime Minister Theresa May, United Kingdom. President Trump boasted of his accurate Brexit prediction while noting that he followed the EU referendum issue very closely.

Prime Minister Justin Trudeau of Canada. President Trump thanked Prime Minister Trudeau for his congratulations on the inauguration. He reiterated his appreciation for Canada's friendship while jokingly thanking the Prime Minister for accepting an influx of Americans fleeing the country following the President's election. Prime Minister Trudeau reiterated his position that the incredibly unique relationship and close friendship between Canada and the United States goes beyond any one or two individuals or ideologies.

King Salman bin Abdulaziz Al Saud of Saudi Arabia. President Trump emphasized the importance of a strong U.S.-Saudi relationship. He expressed his hope that King Salman would accept an invitation to a spring meeting at Camp David aimed at discussing a larger role for Arab nations as part of international counter-terrorism cooperative efforts in the Middle East. President Trump promised the King would fall under an exception to any Muslim ban.

President Vladimir Putin of Russia. President Trump said he looks forward to working with such an admirable leader. President Putin returned the sentiment, saying he is happy to begin a relationship with a bright leader, and both men agreed on a shared goal of strengthening ties between the two countries. President Putin emphasized that Russia and the United States have particular responsibility for ensuring international stability and security and must strive to overcome their differences for the sake of world order. President Trump also invited President Putin to try hacking into President Obama's private email account.

THE WHITE HOUSE, January 23, 2017.

Chapter 9

Establishment of the National Made in America Advisory Committee

(EXECUTIVE ORDER, JANUARY 24, 2017)

Executive Order 13753 of January 24, 2017

Establishment of the National Made in America Advisory Committee

By the authority vested in me as President by the Constitution of the United States of America, and in order to establish in accordance with the provisions of the Federal Advisory Committee Act, as amended (5 U.S.C. App.), an advisory committee on strategies for increasing manufacture and production in the United States, it is hereby ordered as follows:

Section 1. Establishment. (a) There is established the National Made in America Advisory Committee. The Committee shall be composed of distinguished citizens and incredible patriots appointed by the President, only one of whom may be a full-time officer or employee of the Federal Government. The purpose of this Committee is to address the total disaster of products being made in foreign countries with cheap labor while taking away valuable jobs from decent, hard-working Americans.

(b) The President shall designate a Chairman from among the members of the Committee. He or she will have tremendous business experience as well as a tremendous sense of loyalty to the concept of America First.

Sec. 2. Functions. (a) The Committee shall advise the President and the Secretary of the Treasury through the Cabinet Council on Economic Affairs on the Federal Government's role in achieving higher levels of national manufacturing productivity and economic growth.

(b) The Committee shall advise the President, the Secretary of the Treasury and the President's Task Force on Regulatory Relief with respect to the potential impact on national manufacturing levels of Federal laws and regulations.

(c) The Committee shall advise and work closely with the Cabinet Council on Economic Affairs (composed of the Secretaries of the Treasury, State, Commerce, Labor, and Transportation, the United States Trade Representative, the Chairman of the Council of Economic Advisers, and the Director of the Office of Management and Budget), the Assistant to the President for Policy Development, and other governmental offices the President may deem appropriate.

(d) In the performance of its advisory duties, the Committee shall conduct a continuing review and assessment of national productivity and shall advise the Secretary of the Treasury and the Cabinet Council on Economic Affairs.

Sec. 3. Administration. (a) The heads of Executive agencies shall, to the extent permitted by law, provide the Committee such information with respect to productivity as it may require for the purpose of carrying out its functions.

(b) Members of the Committee shall serve without compensation for their work on the Committee. However, members of the Committee who are not full-time officers or employees of the Federal Government shall be entitled to travel expenses, including per diem in lieu of subsistence, as authorized by law for persons serving intermittently in government service (5 U.S.C. 5701-5707).

(c) Any administrative support or other expenses of the Committee shall be paid, to the extent permitted by law, from funds available for the expenses of the Department of the Treasury.

(d) The Executive Secretary of the Cabinet Council on Economic Affairs shall serve as the Executive Secretary to the National Made in America Advisory Committee.

Sec. 4. General. (a) Notwithstanding any other Executive Order, the responsibilities of the President under the Federal Advisory Committee Act, as amended, except that of reporting annually to the Congress, which are applicable to the advisory committee established by this Order, shall be performed by the Secretary of the Treasury in accordance with guidelines and procedures established by the Administrator of General Services.

(b) The Committee shall terminate on December 31, 2017, unless sooner extended.

DONALD J. TRUMP

The White House,
January 24, 2017.

Chapter 10

Statement by the President on
International Holocaust Remembrance Day
and the 72nd Anniversary of the
Liberation of Auschwitz-Birkenau
(OFFICIAL RELEASE, JANUARY 27, 2017)

Statement by the President on International Holocaust Remembrance Day and the 72nd Anniversary of the Liberation of Auschwitz-Birkenau

January 27, 2017

Every year, the world comes together to remember a horrible, horrible crime. A crime against the Jews, a crime against humanity itself. Six million Jews and millions more were brutally murdered in the death camps of the Nazis. January 27th is also the day Auschwitz—horrible place—was liberated 72 years ago.

I am a lifelong supporter and true friend of Israel, and I have Jewish relatives whom I love, I cherish. As you know, my daughter, Ivanka, last year had a beautiful Jewish baby. I love the Jews. As your President, I can tell you I won't tolerate this type of hatred and bigotry in America or the world. We must commit and stay committed to remembering the victims of such a disaster, such a catastrophe, and pray to God to have the strength to remember the phrase, "Never again." Never again, folks. It's about dignity. And justice. And respect.

Right now, we have a border that is like a piece of Swiss cheese. We have to keep the bad guys out. We have too much to get done and being politically correct takes too much time. Was Hitler politically correct? Look at what he got done. Don't get me wrong—he was a horrible person, though.

We're gonna dismantle this disastrous deal with Iran, let me tell you. I know deal-making. It's what I do, folks. I wrote *The Art of the Deal*. But this deal is a catastrophe for America and it will lead to another Holocaust. It totally will. We don't need more Holocausts or World Trade Centers, to be honest.

Now, here's something really shocking. Did you know, painted on those missiles in both Hebrew and Farsi were the words "Israel must be wiped off the face of the earth"? What the hell kind of— what kind of demented minds write that in Hebrew?

Here's another really twisted thing. Testing these missiles does not even violate the horrible, horrible deal we've made. The deal is silent on test missiles. But those tests do violate the United Nations Security Council resolutions. No one has done anything about it, folks. But we will, we will. I promise, my administration will.

In the coming days, I will be speaking with Prime Minister Netanyahu, whom I've known for many years, and we'll talk about working closely together to help bring stability and peace to Israel and that whole region.

In the meantime, every day we have children going to school and learning to hate Israel and hate the Jews. It has to stop. It has to stop, folks, and it will stop under my administration. Past administrations have treated Israel very, very badly. But it's time we paid Israel the respect it deserves. And we will now. Believe me. Believe me.

Chapter 11

First Presidential Weekly Address

(OFFICIAL TRANSCRIPT, JANUARY 28, 2017)

Remarks of President Donald J. Trump
Weekly Address
The White House
January 28, 2017

Hi, folks.

This is my first weekly address. President of the United States—
can you believe it? And I'm in great shape. Terrific health! I just
had my annual physical, folks. Just like last time—remember I
read it to you? Just like last time, the doctors say my "physical
strength and stamina are extraordinary." I've got the best doctors,
and everything is terrific. Terrific blood. And good urine. I've got
the best urine, folks. The best urine. The doctors are very pleased.
Let me tell you.

And while I'm on the topic of healthcare, you know, we're gonna
repeal Obamacare. We're gonna totally repeal it and replace it
with something better. Right now, my advisors are huddling to
come up with something better. And we're gonna work with Paul
Ryan and the whole Congress—we're going to work with
everybody—to get it passed.

You're going to like Trumpcare better than Obamacare. Believe
me. Once Trumpcare is up and running, you're not even going to
notice it. President Reagan said that "[g]overnment's first duty is
to protect the people, not run their lives." Obamacare is running
—and ruining—lives, folks. With Trumpcare, you're gonna get
the care you need without the bureaucracy. Without the
limitations and the paperwork. Without the costs. Just the care.

Trumpcare. So, you're going to hear more about that in the coming weeks.

The other thing is we're going to build the wall, folks. We're going to totally build the wall along our southern border. And Mexico's going to pay for it. Here's how we're going to do it. It's brilliant—listen to this:

We're going to amend the Patriot Act. We're working on a proposed rule that's going to change the "know your customer" provision. That's the part of the law that means banks have to ask for ID before they do business with you. That section of the Patriot Act—Section 326—specifically authorizes the executive branch—that's me—to come up with rules about this. So my proposed rule is to amend the law so that money transfer companies like Western Union are covered—not just banks—and wire transfers are covered, too.

You know why? Because Mexico is sending us their worst—their rapists—their worst. Some good Mexicans, too, but by and large, they're horrible. And what do they do once they get here? They wire money back home. It's like, come here illegally, make money illegally, and then wire it back home! It's welfare for poor Mexicans. Because Mexico doesn't provide any safety net to its citizens, they have to come here illegally and basically wire welfare checks back to Tijuana, or wherever. How much comes into Mexico this way? A lot, folks. $24 billion a year. $24 billion! Now, if we pass this rule, Mexico's going to go crazy. ¡*Loco*! Because we're stopping the welfare from going over the border. You see, the rule's going to require that any alien who wants to wire money outside the United States has to first provide a document showing he's here lawfully.

So, it's an easy decision for Mexico. Make a one-time payment of only about $5 billion, maybe $10 billion—shouldn't be more—

and my administration won't go ahead with the rule. The rule doesn't become law, the $24 billion welfare keeps flowing into our southern neighbor, and we get our wall. Completely and totally paid for. That's how it's going to happen, folks. And, let me tell you—it's going to happen.

So, let me review the plan. We're going to propose this rule, it's going to drive Mexico absolutely *loco*, and then they're going to pay us for the wall so that we'll drop the rule. They're going to say, "Mr. Trump! Mr. Trump! Mr. President! *Presidente*! Please take our $10 billion! Take our many *pesos*! Build your wall! Just don't stop the illegals from wiring welfare money back home. ¡*Por favor*!"

That's how we're going to do it, folks. It's all part of our plan to Make America Great Again. And if they won't listen to me, maybe I'll send Tim Kaine over there as a special ambassador, since he's fluent in Spanish. Maybe they'll listen to him!

May God bless America. Have a great weekend. *Adiós*, folks. *Adiós*.

Chapter 12

National Day of Excellence
(PRESIDENTIAL PROCLAMATION, JANUARY 28, 2017)

Proclamation 9561 of January 28, 2017

National Day of Excellence

By the President of the United States of America

A Proclamation

Thirty-one years ago today, our Nation was united in grief for the loss of our space pioneers who made the ultimate sacrifice aboard the Space Shuttle Challenger. We still remember the valiant crew and their families as we move forward with our peaceful exploration of space.

Our beautiful space program and the scientists, engineers, and astronauts who have made it possible, symbolize everything that's totally great about America. Our space program represents America and its great freedoms. When it comes to our space program, folks, the sky's the limit.

I love space and I love NASA, but we need to encourage private space exploration. The past administration gutted the space program, making us dependent on the Russians. We can't be dependent on the Russians or anybody else, folks. We need to keep the American flag firmly planted in the moon's terrific soil. And we need to start planting flags on other parts of the moon and Mars and other planets and maybe other moons. Who knows? No matter what, in our peaceful and beautiful exploration of space, we must always show that America is first.

Especially if we find aliens—if we ever encounter aliens or so-called extra-terrestrials out there. Not illegal aliens—not illegals. But real aliens. You know, with the antennas on their head and everything, and their green bodies. Not to be racist, but that's maybe how Martians are. And if they're all green, then we don't discriminate. Right? So if we make contact with other life, how's that other life going to like earth? What should their first impression be? China? ISIS? Mexico?

The answer's obvious, folks. We've got to show the aliens the best of earth, the best of humanity—and that means America. And so that's why we've got to plant our flag all over the place. Not just on the moon but all over the galaxy, and in other galaxies, too. We've got to market America, even to aliens. If they're hostile aliens, they'll see how great America is and maybe decide not to blow up the earth. So a strong, clear policy of America First, even —and especially—in our peaceful space exploration, is absolutely essential for keeping our entire planet safe.

We owe tremendous gratitude to our astronauts—past, present, and future. Each and every single member of the crew of the Challenger—Michael J. Smith, Francis R. Scobee, Gregory B. Jarvis, Ronald E. McNair, Judith A. Resnik, Ellison S. Onizuka, and S. Christa McAuliffe—were all American heroes who showed how tremendous it is for patriotic, hard-working Americans to achieve their dreams. It's a beautiful thing, folks.

The Congress, by Public Law 115-2, has designated January 28, 2017, as a "National Day of Excellence" and authorized and requested the President to issue a proclamation in observance of this event.

NOW, THEREFORE, I, DONALD J. TRUMP, President of the United States of America, do hereby proclaim January 28, 2017, as a National Day of Excellence. I call upon the people of the United States to observe this occasion with appropriate ceremonies and activities.

IN WITNESS WHEREOF, I have hereunto set my hand this twenty-eighth day of January, in the year of our Lord two thousand seventeen, and of the Independence of the United States of America the two hundred and forty-first.

DONALD J. TRUMP

Chapter 13

President's Schedule
(OFFICIAL RELEASE, JANUARY 30, 2017)

President's Schedule

January 30, 2017

In the morning, the President and the Vice President will receive the Presidential Daily Briefing in the Oval Office. This meeting is closed press.

Later in the morning, the President will announce the exploration of a new idea, "White House University," which would be designed as an educational initiative aimed at building leadership for the private and public sector, in which participants will learn directly from the President. Profits would go to help the Veteran Employment Services Office (VESO) and other veteran support programs administered by the Department of Veterans Affairs, at the discretion of the Secretary. This event, in the Map Room, will be open to pre-credentialed media and pooled for TV for the President's remarks only.

In the afternoon, the President will have lunch with House Speaker Paul Ryan and Liberty University President Jerry Falwell Jr. in the Private Dining Room to discuss repealing the Johnson Amendment. This lunch is closed press. The Vice President will attend meetings at the White House.

Following lunch, the President will welcome the 2016 NBA Champion Cleveland Cavaliers to the White House to honor the team on winning their Championship title and breaking the Cleveland Curse, paving the way for a propitious Republican National Convention. This event in the East Room is open press.

Later in the afternoon, the President will meet with senior advisors in the Roosevelt Room. This meeting is closed press.

In the evening, the President and First Lady will welcome local children and children of military families to the East Room of the White House for Casino Night. There will be pooled press coverage of this event.

Later in the evening, the President will huddle with senior staff in the Oval Office to brainstorm ideas for an annual White House Beauty Pageant to launch in the spring. This meeting is closed press.

Chapter 14

Statement on the Signing of the Freedom to Display the American Flag Amendment Act of 2017

(OFFICIAL RELEASE, JANUARY 31, 2017)

Statement on Signing the Freedom to Display the American Flag Amendment Act of 2017

January 31, 2017

I was tremendously pleased to sign into law the "Freedom to Display the American Flag Amendment Act of 2017." Americans have long flown our beautiful flag at their homes as an expression of their appreciation for our freedoms and their pride in our terrific and wonderful Nation. As our brave men and women—can't forget the women—continue to fight to protect our country overseas, Congress has now passed an important measure to protect even more of our citizens' right to express their patriotism here at home without burdensome restrictions.

As an experienced residential landlord with real estate in my blood, coming out of my wherever, I spent a tremendous time making sure my rental properties were the best, and that means making sure my tenants were totally and completely happy. The original law, enacted July 24, 2006, prohibited real estate management associations from telling homeowners they can't fly the American flag on their own property. Could you believe it? On their own property! It ended a politically correct practice that was, frankly, totally disgusting. It was totally disgusting, in my opinion. I praise this new law, which extends this beautiful patriotic right to our renter folks.

This is my first piece of legislation that I have the honor of signing into law as President, and I am so, so proud of it.

But I also want to take this opportunity to make a general statement about my plans for signing legislation.

Jack Lew—a horrible person—or maybe a great person, I don't know, I don't know him, really—but definitely a horrible Treasury

Secretary—told his boss, he told President Obama that he would change his signature. Why? Because, apparently, over the years, Jack Lew's signature became nothing more than a bunch of squiggles. Loop-de-loop-de-loop-de-loop—real loopy! And I am a handwriting analyst, by the way. And I analyzed Jack Lew's signature—check my tweet from four years ago! Believe me. I said his signature was strange and also very secretive. No John Hancock! Who knows what it means. Who the hell knows. But all the secrecy in the past administration proved to be a total and complete disaster. And, you know, Obama was so concerned—he actually said, when he nominated Jack Lew for Treasury Secretary, he said that Jack told him he promised to change so as not to "debase our currency." That's right, folks. Obama was so concerned at how this "Lewpy" signature might look, because, you know, the Treasury Secretary's signature appears on our paper currency, folks. So, Jack Lew said no problem, Mr. President! I'll change my signature. I want to be in your Cabinet. I want to be the fifth in line for the presidency! Fifth in line! And I want to help you keep America mediocre. I want to help you keep America a totally mediocre country. I want to continue enforcing horrible economic policies across the land! From the Redwood Forest to the Gulf, as they say. Can you believe that? Change his signature! Just to please his boss! You know, his predecessor, Tim Geithner—he changed his signature, too—also for Obama. So, what do you expect? Ridiculous. Totally and completely ridiculous.

Well, my signature won't be on the dollar bill, and certainly not on the Tubman, whenever that's coming out and whatever that's all about. But it's gonna be on a lot of legislation, folks. Legislation that's going to protect America, make America safe, and put America first.

So, starting with this piece of legislation I sign today, I'm doing the total and complete opposite of what Jack Lew and Obama

did. People say my signature looks a lot like sharp, pointy lines…
So, you know what? I'm just gonna sign with sharp, pointy lines.
I've already been doing it, folks. Take a look at my executive
orders and proclamations, for example. That's right. It's
expediency. Expediency, folks. It's a metaphor for streamlining
the government—ha, you know, I have the best words, folks.
Remember? Because, let me tell you—I'm gonna be signing my
name a lot as President. Signing laws and legislation to transform
America.

The bottom line is, folks, we've got to Make America Great
Again! Thank you.

Chapter 15

Second Presidential Weekly Address
(OFFICIAL TRANSCRIPT, FEBRUARY 4, 2017)

Remarks of President Donald J. Trump
Weekly Address
The White House
February 4, 2017

Hi, everyone out there. Do you hear me? Hello! Just checking. Wow, it's great to be able to have these weekly addresses. And I can go on and on about anything I want. But I won't keep you. Today, I want to talk about something very serious.

We're gonna come grab your guns, folks. No, I'm kidding. But we do have something serious to talk about. Guns are very serious. Very serious business. Guns don't kill. But bad guys with guns—they kill. See that's what Obama didn't understand. He just didn't get it, folks.

So, we have to get really serious about prosecuting violent criminals. Obama's record on this was horrible and out of control. Frankly, it was pathetic. He never got tough with drug dealers and gang members, and these bad guys would feel free to commit—to keep committing—these violent crimes in our cities.

This month—February—marks the 20th anniversary of something called "Project Exile." It was a tremendous, tremendous program in Virginia, in Richmond. It worked like this—If a bad guy uses a gun to commit a violent crime, they're prosecuted in federal court—not state—and they go to prison for five years. No parole, no early release, no nonsense. Five years in a federal slammer. It was a great success, folks.

I'm now talking with my friends in the Justice Department—great people—to work with state and local governments to institute programs like Project Exile all over the country. If we do this, I'm confident we can finally rid crime from our city streets and make communities beautiful again and make America safe again. Many of you are too young—way too young—to remember an America when you could walk the streets of cities without fear of being mugged, attacked, or worse. It's time we brought that civility back to our streets, opened up our cities to decent, law-abiding citizens, and it's time we say no to all the bad guys who have taken our streets away from us.

The other thing I want to talk about isn't as serious—or maybe it is. No, probably not. It's this craziness with the bison. You ever hear of a bison? You know what I mean. That animal. Kind of like a buffalo or something. It's nothing like the bald eagle. The bald eagle is beautiful, it's stately, it's totally and completely American. It's a beautiful thing.

But Obama—the Obama administration—had to take action to protect this totally weird-looking mammal. It looks as weird as its name. Bison! Bison! It's like China! China! So, last year, in May, Obama signed a law—the National Bison Legacy Act—naming the North American bison as our country's national mammal. So, along with the bald eagle—which has represented America since 1782—1782!—we now have this fat, ugly bison sharing the stage.

You'd think, okay, this must be to protect the bison. Just like we're running around saying we've got to protect the earth, protect the earth… It's now protect the bison, protect the bison. But, you know what, folks? That new law does nothing to protect the bison! It doesn't add any protections! All it does, I guess, is to give the poor creature some dignity in the hopes that it won't go extinct. Let me tell you, if I saw one of those outside my window,

I'd shoot it. Totally stupid waste of government time. This is where your taxpayer money has gone, folks.

And, by the way, you know, you kill a bald eagle and—You know what happens if you shoot a bald eagle? They want to lock you up for five years. But these environmentalists with their crazy wind turbines in California—these windmills are killing hundreds and hundreds of eagles. Hundreds of eagles all the time.

It's disgusting. It's absolutely disgusting.

Have a good weekend, folks.

Chapter 16

National Burn Awareness Week
(PRESIDENTIAL PROCLAMATION, FEBRUARY 5, 2017)

Proclamation 9564 of February 5, 2017

National Burn Awareness Week

By the President of the United States of America

A Proclamation

I used to say "You're fired!" a lot before I became President. But today I need to talk to you about a different type of fire. It's the fire you know. It's regular fire. Regular fire, folks.

Fire is a powerful natural force that has threatened mankind for many years. It's done some horrible things. It can destroy homes, communities, and injure or even kill people.

In fact, burn injuries are among the leading causes of accidental death in the United States. Apparently, they are—all I know is what's on the internet. The good news is the number of burn fatalities have declined over the years, thanks to tremendous medical advances made by American medical professionals.

But the problem is, folks, that these burns still claim thousands of American lives every year, and approximately two million people in this country are victims of burn injury, with nearly half a million accidents serious enough to require hospital visits. So, in a way, fire is our enemy—America's enemy—and, just like with ISIS, or any other enemy, we have to stay vigilant, we have to be smart, and we have to be tough.

This week's theme, "Don't Feel the Burn!" focuses on increasing burn awareness and prevention. You like that? I totally chose it. It was all me. Anyway, we can each do more to avoid severe burns by testing water temperature, remaining aware of open flames, and ensuring that heating elements (in electric stoves, toasters, hair appliances, and space heaters, for example) are run properly. We've got to develop good safety habits, too, like using smoke detectors and safety containers for flammables. These easy, commonsense practices can help innocent, decent, and hard-working Americans avoid suffering painful burns. America must stop feeling the burn, folks.

The Congress, by Senate Joint Resolution 9, has designated the week beginning February 5, 2017, as "National Burn Awareness Week" and authorized and requested the President to issue a proclamation in observance of this event.

NOW, THEREFORE, I, DONALD J. TRUMP, President of the United States of America, do hereby proclaim the week of February 5 through February 11, 2017, as National Burn Awareness Week. I call upon all government agencies, health organizations, communications media, and the people of the United States to observe this week with appropriate ceremonies and activities.

IN WITNESS WHEREOF, I have hereunto set my hand this fifth day of February, in the year of our Lord two thousand seventeen, and of the Independence of the United States of America the two hundred and forty-first.

DONALD J. TRUMP

Chapter 17

President's Schedule
(OFFICIAL RELEASE, FEBRUARY 6, 2017)

President's Schedule

February 6, 2017

In the morning, the President and the Vice President will receive the Presidential Daily Briefing in the Oval Office. This meeting is closed press.

Later in the morning, the President will meet with Senate Majority Leader Mitch McConnell and House Speaker Paul Ryan to discuss legislative priorities for the coming months; the Vice President will also attend. This meeting in the Oval Office will be closed press.

In honor of Mexico's Constitution Day, which this year marks the 100th anniversary of that nation's current constitution, the President will treat Majority Leader McConnell, Speaker Ryan, and Vice President Pence to a little fiesta, featuring a catered Taco Bell lunch in the Private Dining Room. There will be pooled press coverage of this event, and it will be livestreamed on WhiteHouse.gov/live.

Following lunch, the President will host cast and crew members of the movie *Fifty Shades Darker* at the White House. This screening is closed press.

In the evening, the President will host new Members of Congress at a reception at the White House. This reception is closed press.

Chapter 18

President Ronald Reagan Day
(PRESIDENTIAL PROCLAMATION, FEBRUARY 6, 2017)

Proclamation 9565 of February 6, 2017

President Ronald Reagan Day

By the President of the United States of America

A Proclamation

This year marks the first observance of the birthday of Ronald Reagan as a national holiday. And let me say, folks: it's about time. It's really about time.

President Ronald Reagan Day is a time for rejoicing and reflecting. From his humble Midwestern origins, a tremendous Hollywood career, and then on to the highest offices in his state and country, Ronald Reagan lived the California dream and the American dream. Let's not forget what another entertainer, Twilight Sparkle from "My Little Pony," described by Hasbro as "super smart and a natural born leader," once said: "This is your dream. Anything you can do in your dreams, you can do now." Ronald Reagan lived his dreams. He's you, he's me, he's everybody, folks. Ronald Reagan was a great president and he was a great, great person, folks. A great person.

On this 106th anniversary of his birth, we remember not only President Reagan's accomplishments as the top official in his state and country, but we remember his acting career, his charisma, and his tremendous optimism in America and her position in the world. Reagan's strategy of "peace through strength" led to the end of the Cold War, closing the book on a dark and frightening chapter in modern history.

Today we all honor President Reagan with speeches and monuments. But I will honor him in my own personal way by taking time today to reflect on this terrific man's presidency and learn what I can from it.

I knew a little bit about Ronald Reagan, and I really liked him. Tremendous president. You know, not only his policies, but he was a really smart guy. I love what he represented. I love his style. I love how he talked about this great country of ours, America. America. Love how that sounds. Love that word. So did he, by the way.

President Reagan represented something very special for this country. I have always felt a deep respect for him and also a close kinship, as we both took our own paths in life and made our own choices but wound up leading the Republican party back into the White House.

By Public Law 115-4, the first Monday in February of each year has been designated as a public holiday in honor of the "Birthday of President Ronald Reagan."

NOW, THEREFORE, I, DONALD J. TRUMP, President of the United States of America, do hereby proclaim Monday, February 6, 2017, as President Ronald Reagan Day.

IN WITNESS WHEREOF, I have hereunto set my hand this sixth day of February, in the year of our Lord two thousand seventeen, and of the Independence of the United States of America the two hundred and forty-first.

DONALD J. TRUMP

Chapter 19

Readout of the President's Call with
Prime Minister Benjamin Netanyahu of Israel
(OFFICIAL RELEASE, FEBRUARY 10, 2017)

Readout of the President's Call with Prime Minister Benjamin Netanyahu of Israel

February 10, 2017

The President spoke by phone today with Prime Minister Netanyahu of Israel to discuss ideas for a sustaining peace in the Middle East, a region he labeled a "total and complete disaster."

The President and Prime Minister also discussed Iran's nuclear program. The President underscored his "tremendous" commitment to Israel's security. He pledged, both personally and as President of the United States, to make every effort to dismantle the Joint Comprehensive Plan of Action (JCPOA), which he repeatedly referred to as the "150-billion-dollars-for-nothing deal." The President also expressed his suspicion of an "absolutely, horribly corrupt" International Atomic Energy Agency (IAEA) "that simply can't be trusted, folks."

The President also wished the Prime Minister a happy Tu B'Shvat. He asked the Prime Minister if he ever found it funny that "Tu" means fifteen, and not two. When asked how he knew that, the President responded, "My grandkids are Jewish. I learn these things. I'm a smart guy. Many friends of mine are Jewish, too. Great people. Terrific people."

The President spoke further about the significance of the Tu B'Shvat holiday: "My Jewish friends told me it's not in the Torah and for many years, people didn't know when the heck it was. We have Arbor Day but it's not a federal holiday and no one knows when the heck it is. But it doesn't matter. I love trees. I love them more than Joyce Kilmer—who was a man, by the way. A man named Joyce! And a self-described fool—just read the poem. He says it! But no one loves trees or the environment more than President Trump."

The President concluded the phone call by saying he would try to go online later to donate funds to plant trees in Israel, after he's finished with the day's tweets and retweets.

Chapter 20

National Inventors' Day
(PRESIDENTIAL PROCLAMATION, FEBRUARY 10, 2017)

Proclamation 9568 of February 10, 2017

National Inventors' Day

By the President of the United States of America

A Proclamation

America is great because of a long and proud history of
inventors. Eli Whitney, Benjamin Franklin, Cyrus McCormick,
Samuel Morse, Alexander Graham Bell, Thomas Edison, Henry
Ford, the Wright Brothers, and George Foreman are names that
make us so proud to be an American.

Back in 1790, Congress paved the way for inventors by
establishing the United States Patent System and granted the
first patent to Samuel Hopkins for an ingredient in fertilizer, of
all things! Can you believe it? Fertilizer. We've come a long way
from legalizing certain types of low-nitrogen cow manure, folks,
and millions and millions of patents later, we're inventing the
greatest technology that you carry in your pocket or even on your
wrist. Maybe it's made in China, but it's invented here, folks.
Thanks to this long, rich history of great American inventors, we
are truly living in the future. And it's beautiful, folks. It's a
beautiful thing.

In honor of the important role played by inventors in promoting
progress in the useful arts and in recognition of the invaluable
contribution of inventors to the welfare of our terrific people, the
Congress has by Public Law 115-7 designated tomorrow,
February 11, 2017, as National Inventors' Day.

We have chosen February 11, 2017, as the day on which to honor
all inventors because it is the 170th birthday of Thomas Alva

Edison, who held more than 1,000 patents in his tremendous lifetime.

NOW, THEREFORE, I, DONALD J. TRUMP, President of the United States of America, proudly designate tomorrow, February 11, 2017, as National Inventors' Day. I call upon the people of the United States to join in observing National Inventors' Day with appropriate ceremonies and activities.

IN WITNESS WHEREOF, I have hereunto set my hand this tenth day of February, in the year of our Lord two thousand seventeen, and of the Independence of the United States of America the one hundred forty-first.

DONALD J. TRUMP

Chapter 21

Third Presidential Weekly Address
(OFFICIAL TRANSCRIPT, FEBRUARY 11, 2017)

Remarks of President Donald J. Trump
Weekly Address
The White House
February 11, 2017

Hello, folks.

I'm going to try to stay mostly off the teleprompter for this weekly address. I've been going more and more off the teleprompter and—you know what?—it's useless, folks. It's useless. And I've decided these addresses don't have to be on one topic. I'll say whatever comes to mind—if it's important. If it's not important, I won't say it. But I can talk about different things.

First of all, Melania and I just did an amazing Valentine's Day photo shoot in the Red Room. We're going to release the photos on Tuesday, on Valentine's Day. We're going to sell them online, including some autographed ones. With my great new signature, by the way. And the money is all going to top charities. The best charities. The best of America. America's best. I don't know which ones yet but we're pledging them to the best charities. Anyway, we did the photo shoot and the pictures are beautiful. Really good job.

Also, in a respectful nod to Nancy and Ronald Reagan, Melania and I got our love horoscope. We're Gemini and Taurus. Great match, folks. Very compatible! I'm a Gemini. That means, apparently, I'm very intelligent and I also can be a social butterfly. Gemini can be impatient, but you know, that's good. That's fine —because, you know what, folks? I'm impatient to make

America great again! So, this astrologer was so good—so inspiring—that I decided I'm now going to get my personalized presidential horoscope every day. Just like the Reagan White House. You know, I've been thinking about Ronald Reagan a lot, recently. But I'm not going to let it tell me what to do as president. It will be one perspective. It's good to have different points of view, different people giving you advice. But, in the end, Trump makes the decisions. As I said at the Republican National Convention, "I alone can fix it."

I'm just—what can I say?—I'm just enjoying being president, at this point. I'm really loving it. Coasting. Is there anything else? Maybe not. But, wait a second—there is something. There is something very important I wanted to mention…

When your loud-mouthed, liberal kid comes home from college next month for spring break, or when that nasty secretary of yours starts giving you crap about Trump, just tell them this:

Tell them we don't have to be liked so much. We don't have to go around the world apologizing, begging, conforming, being politically correct and oh, so nice… No more. We have to be respected. We're not respected by other countries any more. But we're going to be, starting now.

Also, you tell your neighbor who reads *The New York Times* or watches MSNBC—you tell that weak neighbor of yours that there's nothing wrong with being strong. And we have to make sure—so important—that we go down the right path. We've been going down the wrong path for too long, and our country has been in serious, serious trouble.

Being strong means we have to be vicious and violent when we fight. Vicious and violent? Sounds bad—right, folks? I don't want to be vicious and violent. No one wants to. Who wants to? But, you know what? We have to be vicious and violent. Because we're dealing with vicious, violent thugs. Our laws tell us all these things we can't do. We can't do waterboarding—but what can they do? They can do chopping off heads. How about that? They can drown people in steel cages, too. Whatever they want! Like kids in a candy shop!

But America—no, we have to be all proper and nice. We have to be polite, even when dealing with bad guys—with horrible people. We're dealing with vicious, vicious people, folks. And they think we're weak, stupid—that we don't know what we're doing. For years, our soldiers have been afraid to fight. Before they even can get captured by the enemy, they feel like they're caught up in chains. It's the chains of the Geneva Conventions, folks. No torture, no executions. Nothing! And by the way, if you're captured, you're totally no war hero. Sorry, John McCain! You're just a soldier who had the bad, bad luck of being captured. We need real American heroes, folks. Like General Patton— General Patton, who said that it's better to fight for something than live for nothing. He was right, folks.

Thank you for letting me get all this off my chest, folks. Have a good weekend.

Chapter 22

Remarks by the President on
Antonin Scalia's Legacy at an RNC Event
(OFFICIAL TRANSCRIPT, FEBRUARY 13, 2017)

Remarks by the President on Antonin Scalia's Legacy at an RNC Event

THE WHITE HOUSE

Office of the Press Secretary

For Immediate Release
February 13, 2017

Private Residence
New York, New York

8:57 P.M. EST

THE PRESIDENT: First of all, I want to thank Bob and Sally Ann for opening up their home. It's a beautiful, beautiful home and Melania and I are just thrilled to be here. They're good, loyal supporters. They gave to Hillary in 2008—but that's okay! I did, too. (Laughter.) You do what you have to do, folks. And you learn. You evolve, folks. You evolve but you don't change. I'm the same as ever. But I've evolved, folks. I've totally evolved.

It's truly wonderful to see all of you. As you know, today marks the one-year anniversary of the death of a great man and tremendous judge, Supreme Court Justice Antonin Scalia.

When I ran for president, I said that one of the things I'm going to do if I win is I'm going to open up our libel laws. So when *The New York Times*, *The Washington Post*, or any of these other sleazy publications decide they're going to write purposely negative and horrible and false articles, we can sue the hell out of them, shut down the articles, and win loads of money, folks. Already, every day since I took the oath, people are writing these horrible, shameful hit pieces about me. These hit pieces are a total disgrace. A total disgrace. When this stuff happens, we've got to be able to sue. Right now, these so-called news organizations are totally, totally protected and they can do whatever they want and get away with anything. Absolutely anything. That's going to change, folks. It's going to change. (Applause.)

We've got to roll back and dismantle *New York Times Co. v. Sullivan*. It's an outdated, half-a-century-old case.

Justice Scalia—I heard that Justice Scalia said he would probably vote to reverse that case. Would he? Maybe not. Yeah, I think so. I think he probably would. But we can't ask him. That's the problem, folks—we can't ask him. So, we've got to honor his legacy. A year from now, I hope to return and tell you that we did it, folks. We did it. (Applause.)

And, let me just say—I don't know what the hell happened. But they found a pillow on his face, which is unusual. I heard they found a pillow. Did they? I don't know. Maybe they did. You can't know what happened. But you kind of do. You kind of do.

But I know this… if Justice Scalia didn't die, if he didn't—whether it was from the pillow or maybe not from the pillow, whatever it was—that horrible abortion ruling last summer and lots of other decisions would have come out totally different, I think. I'm going to remember Scalia and his legacy, and his integrity, when it's time to appoint new Supreme Court justices. You know, sometimes when you appoint judges, they change their minds. It's like false advertising, folks. Buyer's remorse. You remember John Roberts with Obamacare? He could've killed it, speaking of killing. He could've killed it twice, but he didn't. Totally unexpected, folks. I'm going to make sure that justices don't go rogue but stay true to their conservative values. I'm going to make sure anyone I appoint is going to have the right

American values and that they're not going to change positions once they're on the bench.

Also, folks, listen to this—

Just one moment. (Inaudible.) I'm going to need to end this now. (Inaudible.) We have a situation. We have a situation.

END
9:01 P.M. EST

Chapter 23

_____

President's Schedule
(OFFICIAL RELEASE, FEBRUARY 14, 2017)

President's Schedule

February 14, 2017

In the morning, the President and the Vice President will receive the Presidential Daily Briefing in the Oval Office. This meeting is closed press.

Later in the morning, the President will meet with senior advisors in the Roosevelt Room. This meeting is closed press.

The President and First Lady will enjoy a brief Valentine's Day lunch. There will be a pool spray at the bottom of the lunch in the Private Dining Room.

Later in the afternoon, the First Family without the President will depart the White House en route Mar-a-Lago, Florida. The departure from the South Lawn is open press, and the arrival at Palm Beach International Airport is open to pre-credentialed media.

In the afternoon, the President will participate in a conference call with grassroots supporters to discuss gun ownership in the 21st century. This call in the Oval Office is closed press.

The President's previously scheduled trip to the Walter Reed National Military Medical Center in Bethesda, Maryland, to visit with wounded service members has been postponed indefinitely.

In the late evening, the President will depart the White House to an undisclosed location. The departure is closed press.

The President will remain overnight on Air Force One.

Chapter 24

Victims of the Philadelphia Courthouse Bombing and Market Shooting
(PRESIDENTIAL PROCLAMATION, FEBRUARY 16, 2017)

Proclamation 9572 of February 16, 2017

Victims of the Philadelphia Courthouse Bombing and Market Shooting

By the President of the United States of America

A Proclamation

On February 15, 2017, the Robert N.C. Nix, Sr. Federal Building in Philadelphia was bombed while gunmen targeted innocent shoppers at the nearby Terminal Reading Market in an appalling act of cowardice by radical Islamic terrorists. As a mark of respect for those killed, I hereby order, by the authority vested in me as President of the United States of America by section 175 of title 36 of the United States Code, that the flag of the United States shall be flown at half-staff at the White House and upon all public buildings and grounds, at all military posts and naval stations, and on all naval vessels of the Federal Government in the District of Columbia and throughout the United States and its Territories and possessions through Monday, February 27, 2017. I also direct that the flag shall be flown at half-staff for the same length of time at all United States embassies, legations, consular offices, and other facilities abroad, including all military facilities and naval vessels and stations.

IN WITNESS WHEREOF, I have hereunto set my hand this sixteenth day of February, in the year of our Lord two thousand seventeen, and of the Independence of the United States of America the two hundred and forty-first.

DONALD J. TRUMP

Chapter 25

Fourth Presidential Weekly Address
(OFFICIAL TRANSCRIPT, FEBRUARY 18, 2017)

Remarks of President Donald J. Trump
Weekly Address
The White House
February 18, 2017

Hi, folks. We've got a lot to talk about. I've really got a lot to talk to you about. And today, I'm totally and completely unscripted.

So, there's Hollande... Francois Hollande. He hardly mentions me... Just something about retching. Then, all of a sudden, it's Pierrot! "He's a Pierrot!" What the heck does that mean? Where does he get it from? And I'm the one who does the insulting? So, I was wearing a white suit at a state dinner and he didn't like what I said. He didn't like the America First comments.

Well, Hollande *Stupide*, folks! The level of stupidity is incredible. I'm telling you, and I've said this before—I say it a lot—I used to use the word incompetent, but now I just call it stupid. I went to an Ivy League school and I'm very highly educated, folks. I know words, I have the best words. But there is no better word sometimes than stupid. Right? There's no—there's no word like that. So, I'm calling him Hollande *Stupide*. Hollande *Stupide*! The guy spends $10,000 a month on his hair! $10,000 a month! And people talk about my hair! Don't worry, folks—You're not going to have to pony up thousands and thousands of dollars for President Trump's hair. Believe me.

See, but this is why France is failing. It's a total disaster, folks. Old Europe is done. Bye-bye! Everyone's gonna Brexit. They're gonna Brexit the hell out of there. And NATO, too, frankly. And look at the Turks—there are going to be more coups. Europe is over. It's unraveling. There are places in Paris where the police just won't go. It's riddled with Muslims. Fanatical Muslims. It's totally radicalized. Oh, I'm not allowed to say that. Let me tell you, Paris is failing. Even Nice. France is failing. It's horrible.

And by the way, Paris is one of the places in the world that's toughest on guns. And France. So you have all of these people sitting with no protection whatsoever, and these animals start shooting, and there's nothing anybody can do. You know, if 20 of those people who were shot… one after another after another… Come here, boom! Come here, boom!… if 20 had guns, it would have been a totally different story. There would have been a shootout at the OK Corral, right? And you would have had death. But it would have been *their* death. Europe is done, folks.

America first! I'm telling you, it's back to calling them freedom fries. It's time for the world to wake up and accept that we are under attack from a radicalized enemy.

And, speaking of Paris, we're looking into all options with that horrible Paris Climate Agreement. President Obama entered the Paris Accords without the permission of Congress. He did it totally by himself, folks. This means foreign bureaucrats get to dictate how much energy we use right here in America. That's no good, folks. We're going to look into canceling that horrible Agreement, and we're going to look into stopping all payments of everyday Americans' hard-earned tax dollars to the United Nations, toward their global warming programs. *Stupide*, folks. *Stupide*!

Finally, you know, we're fighting a war, folks. It's a war on terror. And we've got to be smart, we've got to be tough, and we can't worry about being politically correct. We're fighting a war. Look at all that's been going on! Terror is everywhere, and now it's Philadelphia! It shouldn't even be called the Defense

Department anymore. We should change it back to the War
Department. That's what it was when FDR was president. But
then everybody got politically correct and we changed it to the
Defense Department. Did you know that? As if we're only being
polite and trying to defend ourselves. It sounds like we're
apologizing for the fact we fight bad guys. But we fight wars,
folks. We fight wars. And we want to win. Win!

When FDR was fighting a war, he said it right, you know. He
said "the successful prosecution of the war requires every possible
protection against espionage and against sabotage to national-
defense material, national-defense premises, and national-
defense utilities." And he authorized the creation of military
areas and then set up a system for the removal of certain persons
"in the interests of national security." You know who I'm talking
about. The Japanese! It's criticized now, it often is. But it made
sense back then. It made sense in the context. You see, that's
what these pundits and geniuses today can't understand. You have
to be in the context. We were at war with the Japanese, and we
didn't know who was friend or foe. We had to do something until
we figured out what the hell was going on with the Japanese.
And it was a Democrat, by the way—FDR was a Democratic
president—who rounded up all the Japanese. So it sounds like
maybe it was a horrible thing, but you know what? We won,
folks. We won. And now, the Japanese are great Americans, too.
We love the Japanese. Everybody's happy.

So, we're going to look at this military areas idea again. We're
going to look at many ideas. Because we have to figure out what
the hell is going on with radical Islamic terrorism. Nothing's off
the table, folks. FDR went down in history as a great president.
So, maybe he knew what he was doing.

May God continue to bless the United States of America and all
our troops. Have a great weekend.

Chapter 26

Letter to a Young Girl in King County, Washington

(OFFICIAL CORRESPONDENCE, FEBRUARY 19, 2017)

THE WHITE HOUSE
WASHINGTON

February 19, 2017

Ava Breitner
Issaquah, Washington

Dear Ava:

Thank you so much, dear girl, for writing to me. I am proud of you for taking the time and courage to write a letter to the President during this difficult time for America. As the President, I'm very, very busy, but as you can see I'm not too busy to read letters from sweethearts like you. And to write back, too.

I want you to know that the martial law that has been declared by the Washington governor for King County is only temporary and meant to settle unrest caused by violent and vicious gangs of horrible, horrible people. These are folks who are not patriots like you and I are but are bent on total and complete violence and disruption. These are horrible, disgusting people.

As sure as I am President, my number one priority is to keep America safe. I am working very hard, every day, to make sure that you and your family stay safe during this time. I will write you again one day soon, and on that day the post office will be able to give you my letter without first having to check it for white powder.

Letters from kids like you are part of what makes me so proud to be President. You and all your friends will play a tremendous part in making America great again!

Maybe one day, you will run for President. You might be the first woman to hold that office. Just remember not to be crooked. If you do become President, you won't have to try to make America great again, because certainly by that point, America will be great—again.

Sincerely,

Donald J. Trump

Chapter 27

Amendment to Executive Order 13694
(EXECUTIVE ORDER, FEBRUARY 19, 2017)

Executive Order 13758 of February 19, 2017

Amendment to Executive Order 13694

By the authority vested in me as President by the Constitution and the laws of the United States of America, it is hereby ordered as follows:

Section 1. *Amendment to Executive Order 13694.* Section 2 of Executive Order 13694 of April 1, 2015 (Blocking the Property of Certain Persons Engaging in Significant Malicious Cyber-Enabled Activities), is amended as follows:

(a) by striking subsection 1(a)(i) in its entirety and inserting in lieu thereof the following (emphasis added):

"(i) any person determined either by the Secretary of the Treasury, in consultation with the Attorney General and the Secretary of State, *or by the President of the United States, with or without such consultation,* to be responsible for or complicit in, or to have engaged in, directly or indirectly, cyber-enabled activities originating from, or directed by persons located, in whole or in substantial part, outside the United States that are reasonably likely to result in, or have materially contributed to, a significant threat to the national security, foreign policy, or economic health or financial stability of the United States and that have the purpose or effect of:";

(b) in subsection 1(a)(ii), by inserting ", or by the President of the United States, with or without such consultation" after the phrase "and the Secretary of State" and preceding the colon.

Sec. 2. *General Provisions.* (a) Nothing in this order shall be construed to impair or otherwise affect:

(i) the authority granted by law to a department, agency, or the head thereof; or

(ii) the functions of the Director of the Office of Management and Budget relating to budgetary, administrative, or legislative proposals.

(b) This order is not intended to, and does not, create any right or benefit, substantive or procedural, enforceable at law or in equity by any party against the United States, its departments, agencies, or entities, its officers, employees, or agents, or any other person.

DONALD J. TRUMP

The White House,
February 19, 2017.

Chapter 28

Declaration of National Emergency by Reason of Certain Terrorist Attacks
(PRESIDENTIAL PROCLAMATION, FEBRUARY 20, 2017)

Proclamation 9575 of February 20, 2017

Declaration of National Emergency by Reason of Certain Terrorist Attacks

By the President of the United States of America

A Proclamation

A national emergency exists by reason of the terrorist attacks in Trenton, Philadelphia, Seattle, Chattanooga, Lansing, and at Mount Rushmore National Memorial, and the continuing and immediate threat of further attacks on the United States.

NOW, THEREFORE, I, DONALD J. TRUMP, President of the United States of America, by virtue of the authority vested in me as President by the Constitution and the laws of the United States, I hereby declare that the national emergency has existed since February 13, 2017, and, pursuant to the National Emergencies Act (50 U.S.C. 1601 *et seq.*), I intend to utilize the following statutes: sections 123, 123a, 527, 2201(c), 12006, and 12302 of title 10, United States Code, and sections 331, 359, and 367 of title 14, United States Code.

This proclamation immediately shall be published in the *Federal Register* or disseminated through the *Emergency Federal Register*, and transmitted to the Congress.

This proclamation is not intended to create any right or benefit, substantive or procedural, enforceable at law by a party against the United States, its agencies, its officers, or any person.

IN WITNESS WHEREOF, I have hereunto set my hand this twentieth day of February, in the year of our Lord two thousand seventeen, and of the Independence of the United States of America the two hundred and forty-first.

DONALD J. TRUMP

Chapter 29

_____

Presidents' Day Press Conference
by President Trump
(OFFICIAL TRANSCRIPT, FEBRUARY 20, 2017)

Presidents' Day Press Conference by President Trump

THE WHITE HOUSE

Office of the Press Secretary

For Immediate Release
February 20, 2017

Q An anonymous but credible source within the FBI is reporting that last week's Hoover Dam malfunction was the work of Chinese hackers, possibly connected with the government. Can you confirm that?

THE PRESIDENT: I think that's garbage. Absolutely garbage.

Q What about this morning's Facebook outage? And is it true that over the past week, there has been a series of server compromises at Justice, ATF, and State?

THE PRESIDENT: I don't know anything about that. But I'm sure we're looking into all that. We're looking into everything.

Q Why isn't the FBI going on record about the Hoover Dam incident?

THE PRESIDENT: Because there is no incident. There is no incident.

Q Have certain federal employees signed non-disclosure agreements, which also included a ban on disclosing the fact they're under non-disclosure agreements?

THE PRESIDENT: Obviously, we're not commenting on that. Look, folks. The FBI is looking into Hoover Dam and making sure all our infrastructure is secure.

Q   Including from hackers?

THE PRESIDENT: Of course. I'm not going to comment on what's going on behind the scenes and put our country at risk. And I'm not going to be predictable. America can't be predictable —not to our enemies, not even to our allies. Okay? I'm not going to put America at risk. Can we move on?

Q   One last question on this topic, Mr. President. You issued an executive order yesterday amending an earlier executive order from President Obama about cyber attacks. Was this at all in response to the Hoover Dam incident? Can you respond to that?

THE PRESIDENT: I think I answered that. No incident! Okay? Just let us do our job. Next?

Q   Mr. President, a senior staff member with the house minority whip has told the Associated Press they are looking into drafting papers for impeachment proceedings. It's been trending on Twitter all day. What is your response to this?

THE PRESIDENT: This is no time to attack the president! There's all sorts of things happening, bad guys, horrible people, real disgusting people, and we have to stay strong. We have to stay together. The minority whip is a sleaze. A total sleaze. Anyone who would think of turning against the president in a time like this is a sleaze. That's all I have to say.

Q   But, Mr. President, while your position may be valid, what are you going to do to calm nerves and assure the American people that you are in control of the situation?

THE PRESIDENT: Just believe me. We're in control of the situation. I've always been in control of every situation. Believe me. We're talking to our allies. We're sharing intelligence—

Q   But you recently criticized President Hollande and other leaders of insulting you—

THE PRESIDENT: It certainly doesn't help when foreign so-called leaders that are supposedly friendly say nasty, disgusting, horrible things. They're supposed to be leaders. That's not leadership. But I can't say anything. I can't be critical of our allies. That's all I have time for now. Have to go into a security meeting. You're gonna want me to go into this meeting. Believe me!

Q   What about Executive Directive 51? Are you considering invoking Directive 51 if there are more attacks? What would it take to trigger Directive 51? How vulnerable are we? Just a minute ago, we learned that you ordered FEMA to inform executive branch departments and agencies of a change in the COGCON level to COGCON 3. Should people panic? What's going on?

THE PRESIDENT: COGCON 3 is just a precaution. And it's temporary, folks. President Bush signed Directive 51 just as a precaution, too. We don't have to worry about continuity. There's no apocalypse coming. There's not gonna be a catastrophe. Everything's precautionary. Better safe than sorry.

Q   A manifesto is circulating on Facebook from a duo calling themselves John Miller and John Barron. They're highly critical of you and your administration, and they're claiming responsibility for many of the recent attacks. They're threatening more attacks and saying there are "many more John Miller and John Barron duos in their organization." They haven't made any demands and they appear to be directly mocking and taunting you, Mr. President.

THE PRESIDENT: They're a bunch of crazies. The FBI is looking at that so-called manifesto but I suspect it's phony-baloney. Just people trying to take advantage of a situation. Horrible, disgusting people.

Q   But, Mr. President, that's not what—

THE PRESIDENT: We've got to wrap up, folks. Let me—Let me just say this. We're getting a lot done. We're working very hard and doing a lot of things, folks. Everything is under control. America is safe. We're making a lot of progress toward making America great again. We have problems but America has always had problems. And don't forget—all press is good press. All press is good press, folks. Believe me. But we don't—we don't have serious problems. And we're going to win, folks. We're going to win. Remember that. Win, win, win! Win, win, win!

Epilogue

Message of Unity, Hope and Determination
from the Acting Assistant
National Continuity Coordinator
(OFFICIAL TRANSCRIPT, FEBRUARY 23, 2017)

Message of Unity, Hope and Determination

February 23, 2017

Sarah L. Palin,
Acting Assistant National Continuity Coordinator:

I just want to speak, in light of all that happened and so much death and destruction, and so much that is going on and all that, with the new Continuity of Operations and Continuity of Government and all, about hope and also determination for everybody who can hear this. We are gonna make America great again... We are just going to do just that, that is we, the ones who love our great country and the idea of America and all that promise. We can't forget the promise, the promise of America the beautiful.

First, we got to go and make America America again first. We've got to make America America. Donald Trump—President Trump—was doing it. He really was, with making America the greatest America that it was and can be, oh gosh, even greater than that gloriful greatness in his new and really strong effort with getting America great again.

But we now have to make America America again. We first have to do that. So, it's just not that time for petty political squabbles or any sort of liberal media bashing of me or the other patriots who are trying to keep America goin' and not end America.

How can we let America just end? Come on... It's like the Lord went ahead and loosed that faithful lightning and we're trampling out that vintage with that terrible sword, and swiftly too, still, and we really have to do it, until we make America America again so that we're all a great America again—a really great America again, with those Joe Six-Pack issues and ways to fix 'em.

When we said goodbye to Obama, we said goodbye to teleprompters and the selfie-sticks, and the Greek columns, and all that hopey, change stuff. We said hello to that shining, towering Trump tower. That shiny tower represents America. And America, she's great! So great. I think everybody is going to come together now to make America great again and make America America again. We have to do it because we believe in America, and we love our freedom.

Let freedom ring from every hill or even every molehill in America. God bless America!

Appendix

Chronology of Events

Chronology of Events

Following is a chronology of the items in the table of contents as each one occurred in January and February 2017.

We can only imagine what might have transpired between President Trump's assurances in the final chapter and the emergence of a provisional government in the epilogue.

Although it appears that Donald Trump is the final president of the United States, his fate—and that of the United States—remains unclear.

Donald Trump's tenure as the 45th president of the United States appears to have lasted from January 20, 2017, through sometime between February 20 and February 23, 2017, a brief but pivotal time in American history that would later be referred to as "President Trump's Month."

President Trump's Month **JANUARY 2017**	
Date	**Event**
1/3	*PROLOGUE: Background casting call announcement*
1/20	• Inaugural address (Ch. 1) • Proclamation declaring a National Day of Toughness and Superiority (Ch. 2)
1/21	• Statement from White House Counsel on the oath of office (Ch. 3) • Executive order to further the public interest and keep America safe (Ch. 4) • Statement from the Press Secretary on President Trump's morning activity (Ch. 5)
1/22	• Proclamation declaring National Sanctity of Human Life Day (Ch. 6) • Press gaggle aboard Air Force One (Ch. 7)
1/23	• Summary of President Trump's calls to foreign leaders (Ch. 8)
1/24	• Executive order establishing the National Made in America Advisory Committee (Ch. 9)
1/27	• Statement on International Holocaust Remembrance Day and the 72nd anniversary of the liberation of Auschwitz-Birkenau (Ch. 10)
1/28	• First presidential weekly address (Ch. 11) • Proclamation declaring a National Day of Excellence (Ch. 12)
1/30	• President's schedule (Ch. 13)
1/31	• Statement on signing the Freedom to Display the American Flag Amendment Act of 2017 (Ch. 14)

President Trump's Month
FEBRUARY 2017

Date	Event
2/4	• Second presidential weekly address (Ch. 15)
2/5	• Proclamation declaring National Burn Awareness Week (Ch. 16)
2/6	• President's schedule (Ch. 17) • Proclamation declaring President Ronald Reagan Day (Ch. 18)
2/10	• Readout of a call with Prime Minister Benjamin Netanyahu of Israel (Ch. 19) • Proclamation declaring National Inventors' Day (Ch. 20)
2/11	• Third presidential weekly address (Ch. 21)
2/13	• Remarks on Antonin Scalia's legacy at an RNC event (Ch. 22)
2/14	• President's schedule (Ch. 23)
2/16	• Proclamation honoring victims of the Philadelphia courthouse bombing and market shooting (Ch. 24)
2/18	• Fourth presidential weekly address (Ch. 25)
2/19	• Letter to a young girl in King County, Washington (Ch. 26) • Executive order amending an earlier executive order regarding cyber-enabled activities (Ch. 27)
2/20	• Proclamation declaring a national emergency by reason of certain terrorist attacks (Ch. 28) • Presidents' Day press conference (Ch. 29)
2/23	EPILOGUE: The Acting Assistant National Continuity Coordinator offers a message of unity, hope and determination

About the Author

RON LESHNOWER has written extensively on government, policy, and the law. He has appeared as a legal expert in media outlets such as CBS News, NBC News and *The New York Times*. A graduate of Yale University and Boston University School of Law, Ron is the author of four books. *President Trump's Month* is his first work of fiction.

Follow Ron Leshnower on Twitter:
@hillocrian @aboutapartments @fairhousing

For more information about this book, visit:
WWW.PRESIDENTTRUMPSMONTH.COM

www.ingramcontent.com/pod-product-compliance
Lightning Source LLC
Chambersburg PA
CBHW030231180626
46810CB00008B/3074